DISNEY · PIXAR

INSIDE OUT

 phoenix international publications, inc.

When Riley and her parents leave their home in Minnesota for a new life in San Francisco, they're in for a lot of changes! Riley does her best to stay positive, even though she left her best friend and her winning hockey team behind. Help Riley find her way around by looking for these things:

Riley's hockey stick

skateboard

pizza shop sign

street sign

1 HOUR PARKING

Minnesota license plate

DNC 614

bicycle

Riley's Emotions are ready to help her navigate her new city, new school, and new life. With Joy in charge at Headquarters keeping things happy, it seems like Riley can't lose. Can you find these Emotions that reside in Riley's mind?

Joy

Anger

Fear

Disgust

Sadness

When Sadness takes over in Headquarters, Riley starts to feel sad on her first day at her new school. As she tries to fight back the tears, look around and find these school supplies:

these gym shoes

this folder

this backpack

this text book

this lunch bag

calendar

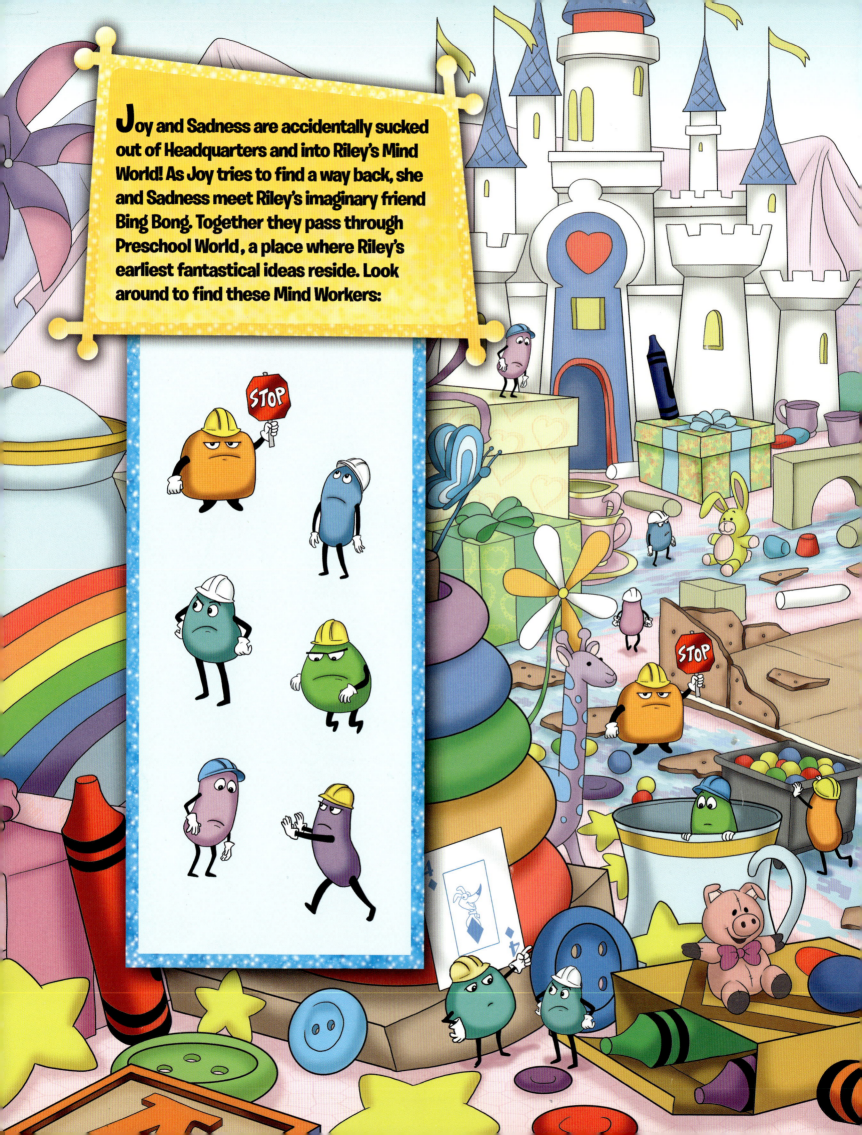

Joy and Sadness are accidentally sucked out of Headquarters and into Riley's Mind World! As Joy tries to find a way back, she and Sadness meet Riley's imaginary friend Bing Bong. Together they pass through Preschool World, a place where Riley's earliest fantastical ideas reside. Look around to find these Mind Workers:

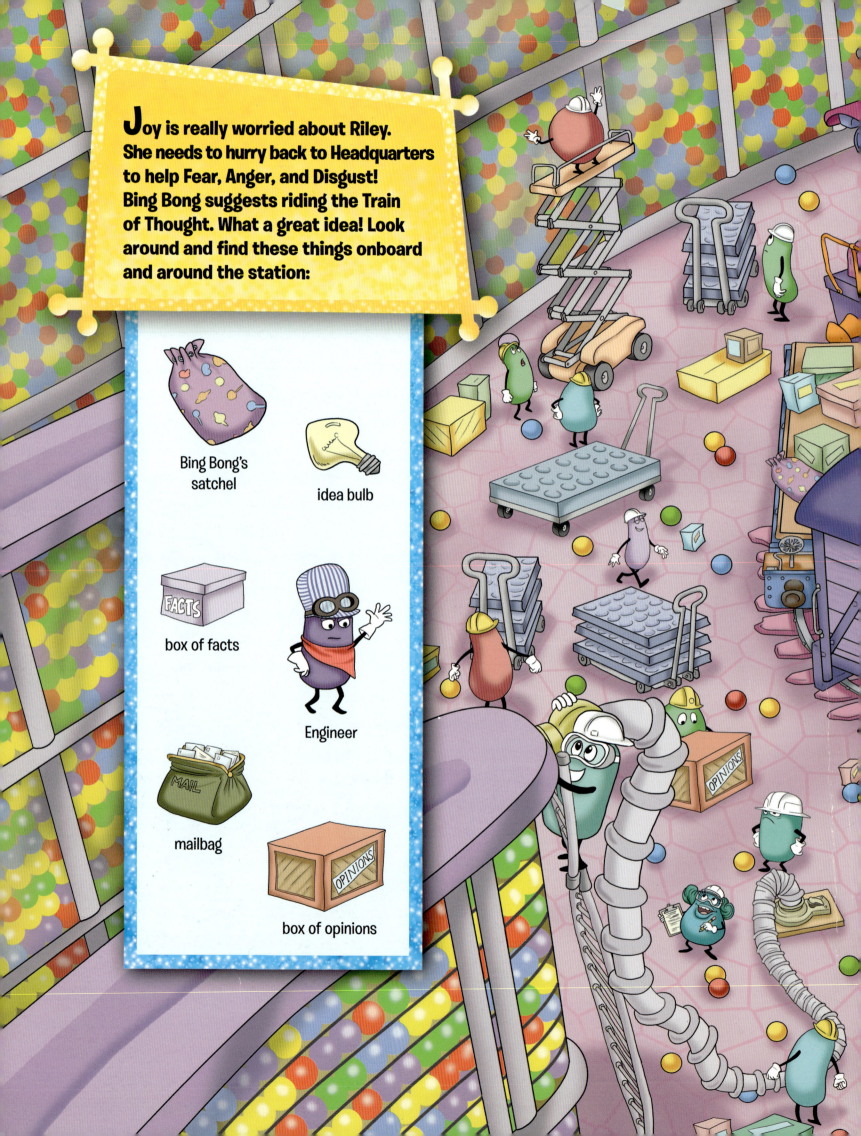

Joy is really worried about Riley. She needs to hurry back to Headquarters to help Fear, Anger, and Disgust! Bing Bong suggests riding the Train of Thought. What a great idea! Look around and find these things onboard and around the station:

Bing Bong's satchel

idea bulb

FACTS

box of facts

Engineer

MAIL

mailbag

OPINIONS

box of opinions

When Riley goes to sleep, the Train of Thought stops running. So Joy, Sadness, and Bing Bong head over to Dream Productions, where Riley's dreams are created. Joy's plan is to try to wake up Riley so the Train of Thought will start up again. Look around for these dreamy things:

megaphone

director's chair

this costume

golf cart

this light

this video camera

Now Riley is awake, but Joy and Bing Bong have become separated from Sadness. They land in the Memory Dump, where memories disappear. Joy is almost ready to give up...but Bing Bong has a plan! While he and Joy try to escape, find these things that Riley has almost forgotten:

jump rope

tricycle

doll

crayons

book

rattle

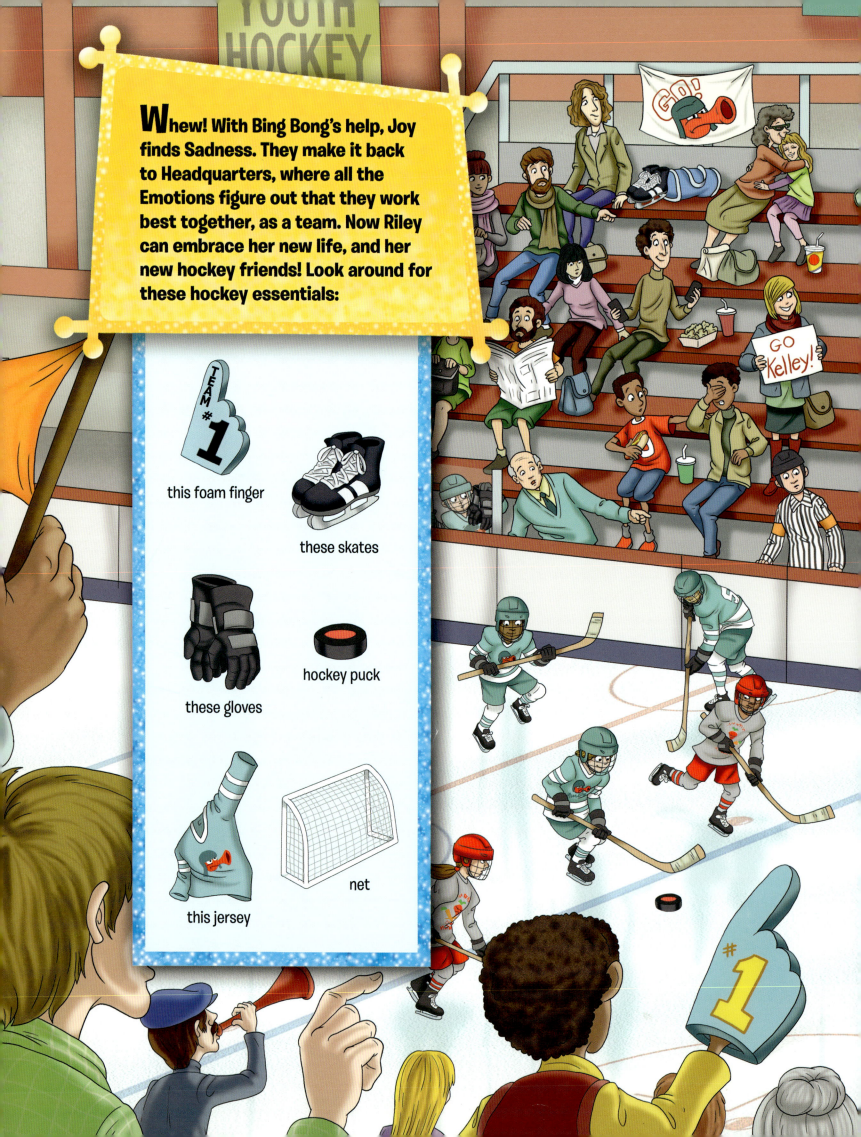

Whew! With Bing Bong's help, Joy finds Sadness. They make it back to Headquarters, where all the Emotions figure out that they work best together, as a team. Now Riley can embrace her new life, and her new hockey friends! Look around for these hockey essentials:

this foam finger

these skates

these gloves

hockey puck

this jersey

net

Drive back to Riley's new neighborhood to find these signs:

873

I ♥ Hockey!

AHEAD ONE WAY

PROTECTED by A-1

Head back to Headquarters and look around for these other things on Riley's mind:

LONG TERM MEMORY RETRIEVAL Vol. 47

Don't be late for class! Hurry back and find these other classroom things:

ERASER

Daydream your way back to Preschool World to find these childhood things:

Hop a ride back to the Train of Thought and look for these things:

This is the stuff that dreams are made of! Return to Dream Productions and find these characters Riley has dreamed up:

Take another trip back to the Memory Dump to find these memories:

Hockey makes you hungry! Find these snacks people are eating in the stands: